First published in the United States 1990 by

Atomium Books Inc.
Suite 300
1013 Centre Road
Wilmington, DE 19805.

First edition published in German, by K. Thienemanns Verlag, Stuttgart-Wien, 1990
under the title "Bennys Hut".
Text and pictures copyright © K. Thienemanns Verlag 1990.
English translation copyright © Atomium Books 1990.

Printed and bound in Belgium by
Color Print Graphix, Antwerp.
First U.S. Edition
ISBN 1-56182-028-8
2 4 6 8 10 9 7 5 3 1

Benny's Hat

Illustrations by Hans Poppel
Story by Dirk Walbrecker
English text adapted by Linda Wagner Tyler

atomium books

One morning Dad forgot his hat.

Benny had always wanted to try the hat on.

As he reached for it,
Benny could see the wonderful ideas inside.

When Benny pulled the hat over his head
he felt a burst of energy.

He kicked the hat over the goalpost
and scored a touchdown.
"I am not a football," said the hat.

Benny cooled down after the game.
"I am not a drinking glass," said the hat.

Benny did amazing magic tricks.
"I am not a rabbit pen," said the hat.

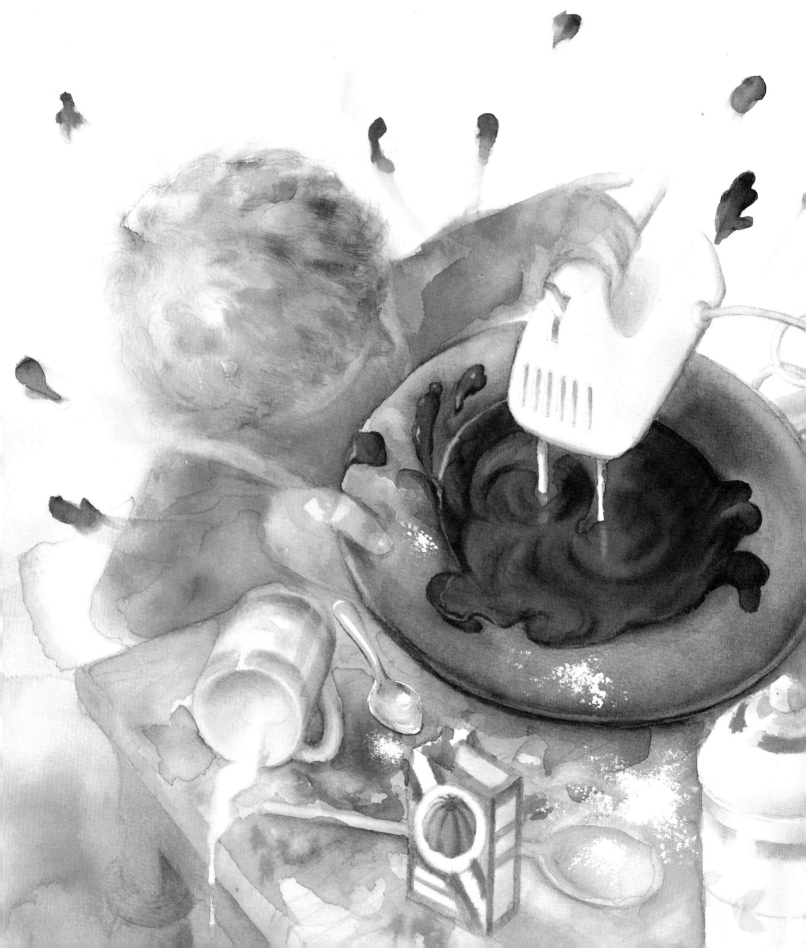

Benny decided to surprise his Mom and Dad
with their favorite dessert.
"I am not a mixing bowl," said the hat.

Benny loved to take baths.
The bubbles had never been such fun.
"I am not a bathtub," said the hat.

Benny snuggled down warm and cosy
after his wonderful day.
"I am not a bed," said the hat.

Dad came in and found Benny.
"I thought I had lost my favorite hat," he said.
"Shush," whispered the hat. "You have."

"I can see I will have to buy myself a new hat tomorrow," Dad said.
Then he gently kissed Benny good night and closed the door.

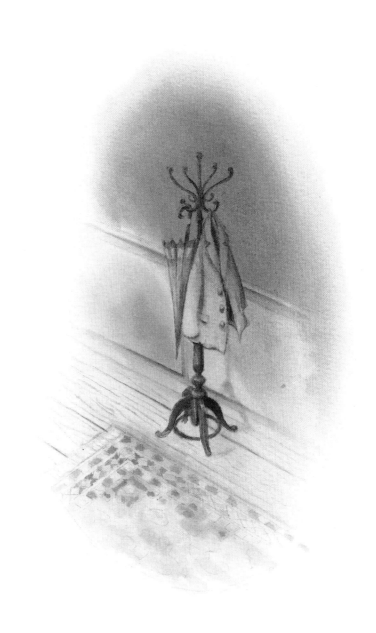